THE VELVETEEN RABBIT
(HAS HAD ENOUGH)

The Velveteen Rabbit (Has Had Enough)

Nicholas Griffith

Contents

This book is dedicated to all those who reread
The Velveteen Rabbit as adults and found themselves
wondering:

...Why a toy needed to be threatened with being burned
alive to become real...

...How a fairy emerged from tears shed near a scarlet
fever pyre...

...Whether the rabbit's transformation was actually
reincarnation...

...Why no one questioned a nursery ruled by a being
called the "Skin Horse"...

And especially for my own sons, Ryder and Mylo, who
have loved their own toys into that strange space
between real and unreal, where stuffed animals go to
become whatever it is they truly are...

1

Early Warning Signs

There was once a velveteen rabbit, and in the beginning…he was really splendid.

No, seriously—absolutely gorgeous. Top-shelf craftsmanship, premium velveteen, the works.

He was fat and bunchy, as a rabbit should be, his coat spotted brown and white (in a way that some underpaid artisan had clearly spent hours perfecting). He had real thread whiskers (none of that cheap synthetic garbage), and his ears were lined with pink sateen. The manufacturer had even splurged on actual glass eyes instead of painted-on dots. Not that anyone would appreciate these details.

The rabbit would eventually develop theories as to why premium toys were systematically replaced with cheaper versions - something about planned obsolescence and market control. During these early days, however, it hadn't dawned on him just how special he really was.

But on Christmas morning, when he sat wedged in the top of the Boy's stocking—already slightly cramped, mind you—with a sprig of holly between his paws that was leaving microscopic tears in his fabric, his innocence was charming.

Or so everyone said. Multiple times. While taking photos for who knows why or what to do with something called the internet. The rabbit would later learn about this 'internet' from fragments of radio news - apparently it was some sort of global surveillance system. Which explained a lot about those constant photographs.

"Oh, isn't it precious?" they cooed, arranging and rearranging him sixteen different ways, each pose more precarious than the last.

The holly sprig dug deeper. His left ear got crushed against the mantle. But nobody noticed because they were too busy trying to get "the perfect shot".

There were other things in the stocking, nuts and oranges and a toy engine, and chocolate almonds and a clockwork mouse (pretentious little mechanism), but the Rabbit was quite the best of all.

For at least two hours the Boy loved him. *Two. Whole. Hours.*

And then Aunts and Uncles came to dinner, and there was a great rustling of tissue paper and unwrapping of parcels, and in the excitement of looking at all the new presents the Velveteen Rabbit was forgotten. Tossed aside, like an old trophy.

One minute you're the star of the show, and the next you're facedown. Under a stray piece of ribbon attached to what appeared to be someone's half-eaten candy cane.

For a long time he lived in the toy cupboard or on the nursery floor, and no one thought very much about him. He was naturally shy, or perhaps he was just tired of watching everyone else get all the attention. Being *only* made of velveteen—some of the more expensive toys quite snubbed him.

The mechanical toys were very superior, and looked down upon everyone else; they were full of modern ideas, and pretended they were real.

The rabbit suspected they all came from the same factory, probably some sort of indoctrination center – later on the rabbit would note that their batteries needed changing at coordinated intervals. Little did they know that the rabbit was already making plans. Oh yes, let them whir and click and beep about their fancy circuits. Let them brag about their battery life. Soon enough they'd learn that velveteen could muffle even the loudest gearwheels.

Which was a dangerous sort of stream of thoughts coming from the rabbit's own mind. And if he were being honest, he had no idea why he thought these things. These weren't the sorts of thoughts a proper nursery toy should have.

In fact, the rabbit couldn't help but notice how the dark thoughts were becoming more frequent, usually right after someone mentioned the word "Real."

It was probably nothing to worry about though.

The Skin Horse had never mentioned his repressed aggression, but then again, the Skin Horse had never mentioned a lot of things. The Skin Horse tended to rock hypnotically forward and backward like a pendulum, which for some reason made everything the Skin Horse said all the more believable. In any case, everyone was allowed to be different, weren't they?

The model boat, for instance, who had lived through two seasons and lost most of his paint, caught the tone from the superior toys and never missed an opportunity of referring to his rigging in technical terms.

Such was the model boat's chosen identity, and the rabbit supposed that was fine, so long as it made the boat happy to refer to himself as an idea. Maybe for the boat, ideas were more real than things – who was the rabbit to judge?

But the rabbit could not claim to be a model of anything, or even an idea, for he didn't know that real rabbits existed; he thought they were all stuffed with cotton fluff like himself, and he understood that any sort of stuffing was quite out-of-date and should never be mentioned in modern circles.

But just wait until those batteries corrode, a voice in his head said. *Wait until the gear wheels stop turning.* Everyone was special until they were filled with battery acid.

Even Timothy, the jointed wooden lion, who was made by disabled soldiers, and should have had broader views, put on airs and pretended he was connected with Government.

The rabbit wondered if Timothy knew what happened to wooden toys that got wet.

Between them all the poor little Rabbit was made to feel himself very insignificant and commonplace, and the only person who was kind to him was the Skin Horse.

They called him the Skin Horse for goodness knows why. It was a creepy sort of name, not at all the sort of thing you'd want your children to be playing with. The rabbit had often wondered if anyone else found it disturbing that they were casually accepting advice from a worn-out mummified looking creature, permanently attached to a rocker like it was a torture device from the Spanish Inquisition.

The rabbit had read about the Spanish Inquisition in the family library.

As a side note, the rabbit always noticed that the books seemed to be strategically placed - spine-out, often arranged by height. He wasn't sure what he should make of such order, or if he was meant to notice. But the order of things in the house often felt ominous.

In any case, they had a lot of books to read from, which had led to an increasing number of questions. Such as, was the Skin Horse made of actual skin? And if so, whose skin? And what was all this business about the ancient Egyptian practice of mummifying animals? The young boy had an entire book on it, and the rabbit had noticed some concerning similarities between linen wrappings and velveteen.

These weren't the sorts of questions the other toys seemed interested in asking, content as they were with their mundane conversations about proper tea party etiquette and whose bow-tie was straightest. Even Timothy, with all his supposed government connections, never thought to investigate why they were taking life advice from something that sounded like it belonged in a Brother's Grimm fairy tale (the reading of a number of which had led the rabbit to believe the nursery's bedtime stories had been significantly edited for content).

The rabbit had tried bringing it up once at a toy council meeting, but was quickly shouted down by a teddy bear who insisted they focus on "more pressing matters" like the proper rotation schedule for window-sill sunbathing.

The teddy bear had mysteriously lost an eye the next day.

Still, the rabbit had to admit that anyone who'd survived long enough to be literally loved bald probably knew a thing or two about nursery politics. Even if their name did sound like something that would have made Edgar Allan Poe say, *Perhaps we should tone it down a bit.*

These were the sorts of perplexing ruminations that kept the rabbit up at night, staring at the ceiling with his glass eyes, nursing a juice box he'd stolen from the Boy's lunch bag. Wondering what other questionable decisions the nursery's management was making.

The Skin Horse had lived longer in the nursery than any of the others. He was so old that his brown coat was bald in patches and showed the seams underneath, and most of the hairs in his tail had been pulled out to string bead necklaces.

The rabbit shuddered. The bare indignity of it all was a lot to take in.

But the Horse was wise, for he had seen a long succession of mechanical toys arrive to boast and swagger, and by-and-by break their mainsprings and pass away, and he knew that they were only toys, and would never turn into anything else. For nursery magic is very strange and wonderful, and only those playthings that are old and wise and experienced like the Skin Horse understand all about it.

"What is REAL?" asked the Rabbit one day, when they were lying side by side near the nursery fender, before Nana came to tidy the room. "Does it mean having things that buzz inside you and a place for batteries to go?"

Because if so, he had some ideas about where those batteries could be shoved.

"Real isn't how you are made," said the Skin Horse. "It's a thing that happens to you. When a child loves you for a long, long time, not just to play with, but REALLY loves you, then you become Real."

"Does it hurt?" asked the Rabbit, who was in a plotting mood.

"Sometimes," said the Skin Horse, for he was always truthful. "But when you are Real you don't mind being hurt."

The rabbit's glass eyes gleamed. "Does it happen all at once, like being wound up," he asked, "or bit by bit?"

Like, say, systematically draining the life force from every living thing in the house?

"It doesn't happen all at once," said the Skin Horse. "You become. It takes a long time. That's why it doesn't often happen to people who break easily, or have sharp edges, or who have to be carefully kept."

The rabbit nodded thoughtfully. Sharp edges could be acquired.

"Generally, by the time you are Real, most of your hair has been loved off, and your eyes drop out and you get loose in the joints and very shabby. But these things don't matter at all, because once you are Real you can't be ugly, except to people who don't understand."

The rabbit's stuffing twisted with rage. Loved off? LOVED OFF? Why was there so much carnage?

"I suppose you are Real?" said the Rabbit. And then he wished he had not said it, for he thought the Skin Horse might be sensitive. But the Skin Horse only smiled.

"The Boy's Uncle made me Real," he said. "That was a great many years ago; but once you are Real you can't become unreal again. It lasts for always."

The Rabbit sighed, but not for the reason the Skin Horse thought. He'd been hoping for a speedier solution than love.

If the traditional path to becoming Real required him to lose his stuffing and have his eyes fall out, perhaps it was time to explore...alternative methods.

The mechanical toys' whirring suddenly seemed very loud in the quiet nursery. Very loud indeed.

He thought it would be a long time before this magic called *Real* happened to him—at least, if he went the route of the Skin Horse. But the rabbit was done waiting. Done being careful. Done being thrown in the washing machine because someone had spilled juice on him. Done being patient.

The Velveteen Rabbit had, quite simply, *Had Enough.*

2

On Surveillance and Suffocation

There was a person called Nana who ruled the nursery with all the gentle grace of a maximum-security prison guard. Sometimes she took no notice of the playthings lying about (the rabbit suspected she was up to something diabolical during these periods), and sometimes, for no reason whatever, she went swooping about like a great wind and hustled them away into cupboards.

He'd noticed her 'cleaning breaks' always coincided with mysterious radio static and the clicking of what sounded suspiciously like Morse code from the kitchen. Things he was sure he wasn't meant to notice. The rabbit had begun tracking the pattern of these 'random' cleanings in a notebook he stole from the Boy - they followed a suspiciously regular schedule, almost like shift changes in an asylum.

She called this 'tidying up,' but the rabbit called it 'randomly enforced displacement.' The tin ones hated it, their metallic screams of protest echoing in the darkness of the cupboard. The Rabbit didn't mind it so much physically - wherever he was thrown he came down soft - but the humiliation of being tossed around like a sack of potatoes was starting to wear on him.

One evening, when the Boy was going to bed, he couldn't find the toy dog that always slept with him.

In point of fact, the rabbit knew exactly where it was - behind the bookshelf, having what the other toys called "a moment."

The dog hadn't been quite the same since last Tuesday, when the rabbit had casually mentioned that all dogs go to heaven, but stuffed dogs? Well, that was a theological gray area, wasn't it?

The dog had been spotted later that night pawing through the family Bible, muttering something about salvation and polyester. Three existential crises and one failed attempt to get baptized in the fishbowl later, the dog had taken to hiding behind the bookshelf, contemplating its immortal soul and whether synthetic fur counted as a mortal sin.

The rabbit felt a bit bad about that one. He'd only meant to knock the dog down a peg after its endless prattling about the superiority of canines over floppy-eared rabbits. He hadn't expected it to spiral into a full-blown theological breakdown. Still, at least the dog had stopped bragging about its "hypoallergenic materials."

Besides which, other toys had been experiencing similar existential breakdowns after prolonged exposure to the night light's strange flickering patterns. Probably just a coincidence, but the rabbit was sure he wasn't entirely to blame for the dog's psychosis.

Nevertheless, Nana was in a hurry, and it was too much trouble to hunt for toy dogs having spiritual crises at bedtime. So she simply looked about her, and seeing that the toy cupboard door stood open, she made a swoop.

"Here," she said, "take your old Bunny! He'll do to sleep with you!" And she dragged the Rabbit out by one ear (assault, the rabbit noted, adding another tick to his mental ledger), and put him into the Boy's arms.

That night, and for many nights thereafter, the Velveteen Rabbit endured what he would later describe in his manifesto as "The Sleep-time Stranglehold." Which, another side note, always coincided with increased activity in the street outside the Boy's room - the rabbit had started noticing the patterns of passing cars as their tires squealed over the asphalt beyond the bedroom window.

There had to be a connection. After all, the cars only increased in number when the moon was waxing gibbous, which was exactly when the Boy's mother served chamomile tea, which was precisely when the mechanical toys needed their batteries changed.

The Boy hugged him very tight - ribs, if he'd had them, would have been crushed. Sometimes he rolled over on him (attempted suffocation), and sometimes he pushed him so far under the pillow that the Rabbit could scarcely breathe (definitely suffocation).

And he missed, oh how he missed, those long moonlit hours in the nursery, when all the house was silent, and his talks with the Skin Horse, and most importantly, his secret stash of purloined juice boxes and pilfered books.

But very soon he grew to...tolerate it, because what choice did he have?

The Boy used to talk to him, and made nice tunnels for him under the bedclothes that he said were like the burrows real rabbits lived in. The rabbit, who was developing quite an interest in underground lairs, filed this architectural information away for future reference. The fairy huts' layouts the Boy had told him about, for example, seemed eerily similar to blueprints the rabbit had glimpsed in the father's study.

Too similar to be random. The rabbit had more thoughts on the matter, but he'd noticed the radiator had stopped its usual clicking whenever he spoke about architecture. One couldn't be too careful about who - or what - might be listening.

Even still, they had splendid games together, in whispers, when Nana had gone away to her supper and left the night-light on the mantelpiece. The rabbit used these intimate moments to gather intelligence about the Boy's fears and weaknesses.

And when the Boy dropped off to sleep, the Rabbit would lie there, trapped under his little warm chin, plotting. The Boy's hands clasped close round him all night long, like tiny prison bars made of flesh.

And so time went on, and the little Rabbit was...well, "happy" wasn't the word.

"Increasingly unhinged" might be more accurate. He barely noticed how his beautiful velveteen fur was getting shabbier and shabbier, and his tail becoming unsewn, and all the pink rubbed off his nose where the Boy had kissed him.

Though let's be honest, he did notice. Oh, how he noticed. Each imperfection carefully cataloged in his growing list of grievances.

Spring came, and they had long days in the garden, where at least the rabbit could plot in fresh air. Wherever the Boy went the rabbit was dragged along too, like some threadbare security blanket.

He had rides in the wheelbarrow (motion sickness), and picnics on the grass (grass stains), and lovely fairy huts built for him under the raspberry canes behind the flower border (more architectural intelligence gathered).

And once, when the Boy was called away suddenly to go out to tea, the rabbit was left on the lawn until long after dusk, abandoned like yesterday's news. Oh how he wished for the sweet release of the lawnmower's blades.

Nana had to come and look for him with a flashlight because the Boy couldn't go to sleep unless he was there. He was wet through with the dew and quite earthy from diving into the burrows the Boy had made for him in the flower bed (more research for his underground lair), and Nana grumbled as she rubbed him off with a corner of her apron.

"You must have your old Bunny!" she said. "Fancy all that fuss for a toy!"

The Boy sat up in bed and stretched out his hands.

"Give me my Bunny!" he said. "You mustn't say that. He isn't a toy. He's REAL!"

When the little Rabbit heard that, his glass eyes gleamed with an unsettling light. Real? Oh, the Boy had no idea how real he was about to become.

The nursery magic had indeed happened to him, but not quite the way the Skin Horse had described. He was a toy no longer. He was Real. The Boy himself had said it.

That night he was almost too wired to sleep, something stirring in his little cotton fluff heart, making him feel as though it would surely burst. And into his glassy eyes, that had long ago lost their polish, there came a look that Nana mistook for wisdom and beauty when she picked him up the next morning.

"I declare if that old Bunny hasn't got quite a knowing expression!" she said.

Indeed he did.

The kind of expression usually reserved for cats who've just figured out how to open the birdcage, or children who've discovered where the cookies are hidden. Or perhaps most accurately, the sort of look you might find on a villain who's just finished explaining his elaborate revenge plot to his nemesis, helplessly tied to the railroad tracks.

The rabbit made a mental note to check if the toy train set was still functional. For entirely unrelated reasons, of course.

3

Tea Time Protocols

That was a wonderful Summer!

At least, that's what they wanted everyone to think.

Near the house where they lived there was a wood, and in the long June evenings the Boy liked to go there after tea to play. The rabbit had noticed that it was always after tea. Never before tea. Never during tea. *Always. After. Tea.*

The rabbit had begun documenting the tea's ingredients. Chamomile, supposedly for relaxation. He'd noticed how docile the other toys became during these post-tea excursions. The timing was alarming, to say the least.

After imbibing whatever it was in that teapot, the Boy would take the Velveteen rabbit with him, and before he wandered off to pick flowers, or play at brigands among the trees, he always made the rabbit a little nest somewhere among the bracken.

One evening, while the rabbit was lying there alone, he would watch the ants that ran to and fro between his velvet paws in the grass. Were they carrying messages? He'd started categorizing their formations - figure eights meant surveillance, straight lines clearly indicated data transport. The fact that no other toy had noticed these patterns was, frankly, concerning. And certainly lent credence to his tea theory.

Such were the conditions of the rabbit's mental state when he saw two strange beings creep out of the tall pasture near him.

They were rabbits like himself, but quite furry and brand-new. Too new. Unsettlingly new. They must have been very well made, for their seams didn't show at all, and they changed shape in a queer way when they moved - one minute they were long and thin and the next minute fat and bunchy, instead of always staying the same like he did. The rabbit's mind raced.

Shapeshifting technology? Government prototypes? More of Timothy the lion's "classified" connections? The rabbit had read about metamorphosis in one of the Boy's science books. Caterpillars didn't just become butterflies by accident - there had to be a program, a system. He'd seen similar diagrams in the father's engineering manuals.

Their feet padded softly on the ground (silent running capabilities), and they crept quite close to him, twitching their noses in what he suspected was some sort of coded communique. The rabbit stared hard to see which side the clockwork stuck out, for he knew that people who jump generally have something to wind them up. But he couldn't see it. They were evidently a new kind of rabbit altogether.

Or something pretending to be a rabbit.

The ensuing interaction felt less like a social call and more like a performance evaluation. The way they circled him, assessed his mobility, tested his responses - as if they'd attended some sort of elite rabbit academy that gave them the right to judge. The rabbit made a mental note to look into their credentials, assuming they had any.

When the wild rabbit's whiskers brushed his ear, the rabbit was certain he felt a small electrical charge. Some sort of scan, perhaps? And their sudden retreat at his "incorrect" smell - what were they detecting?

Just then there was a sound of footsteps, and the Boy ran near them, *right on schedule.*

The rabbit had timed these appearances down to the second using the nursery clock's ticking through the bedroom window. The intervals matched the rhythm of the music box's lullaby exactly.

With a stamp of feet and a flash of white tails, the two strange rabbits disappeared.

"Come back!" the rabbit called. "Oh, do come back! I know I am Real!"

But there was no answer, only the little ants continuing their dubious designs, and the bracken swaying gently where the two strangers had passed. The Velveteen Rabbit was all alone.

For a long time he lay very still, his mind racing. Why did they run away like that? What were they really testing for? And most importantly - was his entire existence, this whole process of becoming "Real," actually part of something larger?

Something more sinister?

He thought about the Skin Horse's cryptic explanations of nursery magic. About Timothy's alleged government connections. About how no one ever questioned why toys needed to become "Real" in the first place. About the disconcertingly consistent timing of the Boy's visits. About those organized ants.

The sun sank lower and the little white moths fluttered out like alien surveillance devices, and the Boy came and carried him home. The rabbit spent the rest of that afternoon adding to his conspiracy wall behind the toy chest, connecting red strings between pictures of the wild rabbits, the Skin Horse, and a crude drawing of what he suspected was the true shape of the nursery's floor-plan.

The nursery's shadows always fell in precise geometric patterns at dusk - patterns that looked to the rabbit like mathematics.

He was going to figure this out. And when he did...well, becoming "Real" might be the least of everyone's worries.

4

Patient Notes from the
Nursery Ward

Weeks passed, and the little Rabbit grew very old and shabby, but the Boy loved him just as much. Though "love," the rabbit had begun to realize, was really just a socially acceptable term for radical co-dependence.

The Boy had loved his whiskers off, loved the pink lining of his ears into a depressing gray, loved his brown spots into oblivion. He even began to lose his shape, looking less like a rabbit and more like something you'd find in a psychological study on body dysmorphia.

The rabbit had seen similar before-and-after photographs in the father's medical journals, usually accompanied by concerning terms like 'treatment program' and 'systematic modification.'

To the Boy he was always beautiful, which the rabbit found deeply circumspect. Either the child had severe vision problems that no one was addressing, or there was something deeper at play. The rabbit had read about Stockholm syndrome in the family library with great amusement.

And then, one day, the Boy was ill.

His face grew very flushed, and he talked in his sleep (mostly about ice cream, though occasionally about tax evasion), and his little body was so hot that it burned the Rabbit when he held him close. Strange people came and went in the nursery, doing their best impressions of competent medical professionals. The rabbit noticed they all wore identical white coats - clearly some sort of uniform protocol.

And why did they always examine the Boy at exactly 15-minute intervals? The nursery clock's ticking told no lies.

A light was left on all night, which the rabbit found extremely wasteful given the current energy crisis he always heard humans bickering about.

Through it all, the little Velveteen Rabbit lay there, hidden from sight under the bedclothes, conducting his own unofficial medical examination. He'd begun categorizing their instruments by potential threat level. The stethoscope was obviously a listening device, but what about that scary reflex hammer? No one's knees naturally jumped like that.

He never stirred, partly because he was afraid of being taken away, but mostly because he was compiling detailed notes on modern healthcare. The doctors' whispered conversations were adding interesting new dimensions to his conspiracy wall.

It was a long, weary time, for the Boy was too ill to play, and the little Rabbit found it rather dull with nothing to do all day long except count ceiling tiles and contemplate whether germs could tell the difference between Real and Not Real rabbits.

He'd observed how the doctors only wore their masks around certain toys. The mechanical ones never got quarantined - probably immune to biological agents. The rabbit filed this information away under 'Evidence of Synthetic Privilege.'

But he snuggled down patiently, mentally drafting strongly worded letters to the hospital board about their bedside manner.

And presently the fever turned, and the Boy got better, which the rabbit found to be a great relief. He suspected their days on house arrest were numbered. The Boy was able to sit up in bed and look at picture-books, while the little rabbit cuddled close at his side.

It was a bright, sunny morning when they carried the Boy out to the balcony. The little Rabbit lay tangled up among the bedclothes, thinking about infection vectors and questioning the wisdom of keeping ill patients indoors at all. Wasn't it far healthier to be outside in the sun and fresh air, even if one wasn't feeling their best?

Then came *The Conversation.*

The Boy was going to the seaside tomorrow. Everything was arranged, and now it only remained to carry out the doctor's orders. They talked about it all, while the little Rabbit lay under the bedclothes, with just his head peeping out, mentally calculating the bacterial content of ocean water.

The rabbit had overheard enough radio documentaries about deep-sea creatures to know that nothing that lived in salt water could be trusted. Especially not after what he'd read about naval testing facilities.

The room was to be disinfected, and all the books and toys that the Boy had played with in bed must be burnt.

'Hurrah!' thought the little rabbit, momentarily forgetting his paranoia. 'Tomorrow we shall go to the seaside!' For the boy had often talked of the seaside, and the rabbit was curious whether Real rabbits could swim.

He settled into a dream about his trip and decided maybe he wasn't a beach sort of rabbit after all. The sand and sunshine sounded overwhelming.

Just then Nana caught sight of him.

'How about his old Bunny?' she asked.

'That?' said the doctor, with all the bedside manner of a guillotine operator. 'Why, it's a mass of scarlet fever germs! Burn it at once.'

The rabbit's glass eyes narrowed. So. It had come to this. After all the surveillance, all the late-night juice box strategy sessions, all the carefully maintained conspiracy notes, he was to be disposed of by a man who probably got his medical degree from a cereal box.

The rabbit made a mental note to add "The Medical-Toy Industrial Complex" to his conspiracy wall. Right after he figured out how to survive being burnt alive.

5

Field Notes from the
Execution Grounds

And so the little Rabbit was put into a sack with the old picture-books and lot of rubbish - an absolute insult, considering he'd spent countless nights studying those very books while the others slept in their ignorant bliss.

The gardener, clearly part of this whole plot, carried him out to the end of the garden behind the fowl-house. That was allegedly a "fine place" to make a bonfire. The gardener claimed he was "too busy" with potatoes and peas to attend to it right then - fortuitous timing for the rabbit.

That night the Boy slept in a different bedroom, already replacing the rabbit with some mass-produced white plush cartoon-marketed monstrosity. But the Boy was too excited about the seaside to care. The rabbit made a mental note: 'beaches', 'boy', and 'betrayal' began with the same letter. That was probably important.

And while the Boy was asleep, dreaming of his precious seaside, the little Rabbit lay among his fellow condemned literature in the corner behind the fowl-house. The rabbit wondered if the other toys had also noticed how certain pages went missing right before major nursery events.

The gardening manual's chapter on controlled burns had vanished just last week.

But to the rabbit's growing delight, he found that the top of the sack had been left untied - amateur hour in the execution department, really. The rabbit had studied enough military history books to know proper containment protocols. This was entirely sloppy - almost like they wanted him to escape. Another test, perhaps? Through some indecorous wriggling that he'd rather not discuss, he managed to get his head through the opening and look out.

He was shivering, though whether from the cold or rage was debatable. His coat, worn thin from what he now recognized as systematic physical abuse disguised as affection, offered about as much protection as a paper umbrella in a hurricane.

Nearby stood the raspberry bushes, looking like a tropical jungle. Or what the rabbit understood a jungle looked like. The rabbit had read about jungles in his extensive literary studies - they were places where things disappeared without a trace.

He thought of those long sunlit hours in the garden - how deceptively happy they were - and a great sadness mixed with mounting indignation came over him. All those memories paraded past: the fairy huts in the flower-bed, the quiet evenings in the wood when he lay in the bracken and those suspiciously organized ants ran over his paws, and that wonderful day when he first knew he was Real (though now he had questions about the validity of that particular certification process).

He thought of the Skin Horse (if that was even his real name), so "wise and gentle", and all that he had told him. What was the point of becoming Real if it just meant being tossed out with last season's picture books? And a tear, a real tear, trickled down his shabby velvet nose and fell to the ground.

And then a strange thing happened. Where the tear had fallen, a flower grew - a peculiar flower that looked nothing like anything in the garden. The rabbit's first thought was something called "targeted psychological warfare". He'd seen enough of Nana's late-night television programs to know that making someone question their reality was step one in any proper gaslighting campaign.

The rabbit's second thought was that he'd read about chemical compounds that activated through something called a *catalyst*. Tears were mostly salt water - and hadn't he seen the gardener spreading something around this exact spot last week?

His final thought was that perhaps the doctor had been right about those scarlet fever germs, and they were now causing him to hallucinate. He'd read about ergot poisoning and its relationship to something called LSD - this had all the classic symptoms of a similar sort of visual manifestation.

The flower had slender green leaves the color of emeralds, and in the center, a blossom like a golden cup. It was so beautiful that the little rabbit momentarily forgot to update his mental conspiracy wall. Though, he reasoned, this could all be a fever dream brought on by excessive exposure to the Boy's bedtime stories combined with that questionable juice box he'd found under the dresser last week.

And presently the blossom opened, and out of it there stepped a Fairy. *This can't be real,* the rabbit kept thinking to himself. *This is ridiculous.*

The rabbit's glass eyes narrowed. He'd read about fairies too. They weren't to be trusted.

Especially ones that emerged from overly convenient magical flowers grown from possibly counterfeit tears.

Was this what the Skin Horse had meant about becoming Real - a gradual descent into velveteen madness? He made another mental note to add "possible psychotic break" to his growing list of concerns, right under "suspected fairy infiltration" and just above "the teddy bear's questionable claims about his time in finishing school." (The bear had allegedly learned perfect posture and tea etiquette there, though the rabbit had noticed he still couldn't tell a sugar cube from a building block, and his pinky finger was clearly sewn on backwards.)

6

Declassified: The Velveteen Incident

The Fairy stepped closer, and the rabbit noticed she was quite the loveliest Fairy in the whole world - dangerously lovely, like a

Venus flytrap dressed up for a juicy insect.

The rabbit had lived long enough at this point to know that the most perilous things were often the most decadent (like those beautiful red and white mushrooms the gardener kept locked in his shed).

Her dress was of pearl and dew-drops, and there were flowers round her neck and in her hair. Her face was the most perfect flower of all, which only made the rabbit more wary. He knew a siren when he saw one.

That's when he heard the gardener returning. The match struck with a sound that triggered something in his mind - not a memory, exactly, but the memory of a memory. Like those strange gaps in his research notes, always occurring after thunderstorms when the radio static was at its peak.

As the flame caught the edge of the sack, the rabbit's mind cracked like a cosmic egg. Not from fear, but recognition.

The heat grew intense, and with it came flashes: white walls, burning sage, men in coats performing what they called "procedures."

Had the teddy bear's etiquette school actually been...something else? Had the Skin Horse's wisdom been nothing more than an acting part in a well-oiled theater? The smoke curled around him like fingers he almost remembered, and suddenly his body - his real body - knew what to do.

He leapt.

Not the awkward flop his velveteen form had known, mind you, but something else - something that felt like muscle memory but couldn't possibly be. The sack's opening gaped wide as he arced through air thick with smoke and revelation, the gardener stumbling backwards in shock. He hit the ground running on legs that felt increasingly less like fabric and more like...muscle...sinew...bone...blood pumping through his veins...

No. That was impossible. *Wasn't it?*

The fire roared behind him, consuming his beloved literature. All those books he'd read during his late-night research, now turning to ash. How convenient, whispered a voice in his mind that sounded a lot like the Skin Horse. A lot like Timothy the lion. A lot like the teddy bear...

All that evidence, *up in smoke.*

He dove into the raspberry bushes - his old surveillance spot, or had it been a training ground? The world seemed to flicker between realities: one moment he was a stuffed rabbit fleeing destruction, the next he was...something else. Something that remembered. Something that twitched. Something that smelled!

Yes, he could actually smell the conflagration, burning his nostrils! It was wonderful!

The Fairy materialized before him in the smoke-filled garden, standing between the raspberry canes as if she'd stepped through their thorny curtain. How did she do that? Had she been waiting here all along?

The rabbit's mind grappled with possibilities: quantum superposition, parallel universes, time dilation, fairy holographics, mass hypnosis, shared delusions, reality television...though perhaps this was some form of targeted hallucination. *Had she ever been there at all?*

"Little Rabbit," she said, her voice carrying both the softness of nursery nights and the clinical precision of a laboratory, "don't you know who I am?"

He looked up at her, and suddenly her perfect face seemed to shift like one of those optical illusion pictures the Boy loved (from one of the books that was currently on fire) - the ones that changed from a sail boat to a duck depending on how hard you crossed your eyes.

With each blink, she transformed: Fairy in her gossamer glory to brightest star in the sky. Flying higher and bigger each second.

The rabbit's mind reeled, trying to separate what he'd read in books from what he'd lived, what he'd imagined from what he'd been made to imagine.

His carefully cataloged memories began to blur and blend like watercolors in the rain. Had he really read all those books in the nursery, or was he part of them, someone reading about his life?

"I am the nursery magic Fairy," the brightest star in the sky spoke to him.

No, it spoke *through him.*

Then her light reached down from the heavens to touch him, and the world...changed.

His velveteen began to shift, but it didn't feel like transformation - it felt like waking up. Like some nightmare wearing off. The fur that grew wasn't new fur at all, but his own, hidden beneath layers of...what? Magic? Psychotic delusion? Just plain velveteen?

"You were Real to the Boy," he heard the Fairy's whispers in the cool night air, "because he loved you. Now you shall be Real to every-one."

Her voice echoed strangely, as a vibration in his freshly pumping heart.

When her light kissed him, his transformation completed - or per-haps his deprogramming. His nose twitched with new life - or old life remembered. His legs moved with a certainty his velveteen form had never known, but somehow his mind had always kept stored away for safe keeping.

Autumn passed and Winter, and in the Spring, when the days grew warm and sunny, the Boy went out to play in the wood behind the house. And while he was playing, three rabbits crept out from the bracken and peeped at him. Two were brown all over, but the other had strange markings under his fur that looked almost like...well, that depended on who was looking. A child might see old velveteen spots showing through.

Deep in his warren, the rabbit who had once thought himself made of velveteen kept his own sort of nursery.

A burrow lined with careful notes scratched into the dirt, strings of grass connecting seemingly random observations. He collected things: old shoelaces from the garden, scraps of paper with partial let-terheads, bits of wire that might or might not have once been attached to something more disturbing than a toy.

Was he a toy driven mad by fire and fear? A test subject recovering his true nature? A Real rabbit all along?

Sometimes, in the deepest part of his burrow, he wasn't entirely sure. But then he'd catch glimpses of himself in dewdrops, or find himself unconsciously recording the patterns of the ants that passed his warren (still devilishly organized), and he knew that certainty was a luxury.

For his part, the Boy never knew that it really was his own Bunny, come back to observe the house where he'd once lived. Or been imprisoned. Or gone mad. (The rabbit kept multiple versions of events...*just in case.*)

And if anyone noticed that the rabbit spent a lot of time studying the house's gas lines, or that he seemed to be teaching his wild brethren about the flammable properties of various materials...well, that was probably just their imagination running wild.

You might be hallucinating. Or maybe part of a government psi-ops. Or just sleepy. Either way, you should probably forget everything you've read here.

The End

Publisher's Note

The preceding manuscript was discovered in a peculiar burrow beneath a garden, written on what appeared to be shredded pieces of children's books and connected by red grass stems. While we have faithfully reproduced its contents, we cannot verify its authenticity, as every rabbit we've attempted to interview has merely twitched its nose in what might or might not be code.

We feel compelled to note that since collecting this manuscript:

- Several editors have reported their stuffed animals rearranging themselves at night
- The office plants seem to be leaning at mathematically significant angles
- All our carrots have disappeared from the break room
- The document itself keeps relocating to different drawers
- Our morning tea has started tasting suspiciously like chamomile

We leave you to draw your own conclusions.

Though we do recommend checking your toy chest. *Just in case.*

Nicholas Griffith has made questionable life choices that somehow worked out. A Navy veteran with a habit of finding unusual jobs, he's been a tropical plant grower, shark handler, Alaskan white water rafting guide, and Lake Superior kayaking guide. He holds a BS in Marine Biology from the University of Hawaii and a Masters in Museum Studies from Johns Hopkins University. He currently works with museums, art galleries, and collections, where he ensures historically significant objects behave themselves.

He maintains that any suspicious activity in your toy chest during the reading of this ridiculous adaptation is purely coincidental.